D0833619

# EVERYTHING TO LIVE FOR

## A Story From Northern Ireland

*Look out for other titles in the Survivors series:*

The Beat of a Drum – A Story of African Slavery

Boxcar Molly – A Story From the Great Depression

Broken Lives – A Victorian Mine Story

The Enemy – A Story From World War II

False Papers – A Story From World War I

Long Walk to Lavender Street – A Story From South Africa

Only a Matter of Time – A Story From Kosovo

The Star Houses – A Story From the Holocaust

The Water Puppets – A Story From Vietnam

SURVIVORS

# EVERYTHING TO LIVE FOR

*A Story From Northern Ireland*

Stewart Ross

*an imprint of Hodder Children's Books*

Book editor: Katie Orchard

Published in Great Britain in 2002 by Hodder Wayland
An imprint of Hodder Children's Books Limited



British Library Cataloguing in Publication Data

Ross, Stewart
Everything to Live For: a story from Northern Ireland – (Survivors)
1. Northern Ireland – History
2. Children's stories
I. Title
823.9'14 [J]

ISBN 0 7502 3360 5

The publishers would like to thank the following for permission to reproduce their photographs on the cover:
Angela Hampton Family Life Picture Library;
Photofusion © Vehbi Koca; Popperfoto.

Typeset by Avon Dataset Ltd, Bidford-on-Avon, Warks
www.avondataset.com

Printed and bound in Great Britain by
Clays Ltd, St Ives plc

# Introduction

Part of Ireland has been more or less under British rule for more than 800 years. In the seventeenth century, thousands of Protestants from England and Scotland settled in the northern part of the island, known as Ulster. They developed their own culture and way of life, and were fiercely hostile to the country's Roman Catholic majority.

When Ireland became an independent country in 1922, Ulster refused to join with it and remained part of Great Britain. Many Irish people resented this, and hoped one day to unite Ulster with the rest of Ireland (Eire). Meanwhile, the Protestant majority in Ulster severely discriminated against the Catholic minority. In 1968 Catholic civil rights protests sparked violent riots and the British army was sent in to keep the peace.

So began the latest phase of the 'Troubles' – more than thirty years of civil violence that sometimes spilled over into mainland Britain. Militant Catholics ('terrorists' or 'freedom fighters', depending on one's point of view) in the Provisional IRA and other groups tried to drive the

British from Northern Ireland by force. Their main tactics were shootings and bombings. Protestant paramilitary groups responded in a similar manner. The police, the British army and the great majority of peace-loving citizens were caught between the two groups.

Finally, at Easter 1998 after years of negotiations, the British and Irish governments put forward an agreement for a lasting cease-fire and political settlement. However, it was not to the liking of all the paramilitaries...

*Everything To Live For* is fiction. The precise settings and the characters are all made up. Nevertheless, it is closely based on a real event – the detonation of a massive bomb in the High Street of the town of Omagh on Saturday 15 August 1998.

I would like to express my sincere thanks to Dr Mike Wain, Matthew Costecalde and Ellie Ross for their invaluable contributions and assistance.

Dedicated to Jacqui Pick and the pupils of the Croydon Advisory Services' Summer School in Creative Writing for Talented and Able Pupils, 2001: Helen Burch, Nadelia Burke, Louise Flower, Polly Howells, Andy Lancaster, Ewan Miller, Sean Rudder, Mabel Ogakwu, Keeley Boyle, Anna Collins, Francesca Docherty, Hayley Kearns, Katherine MacArdle, Hurmus Oltan, Lewis Stawman, Jade Brown and Vaneeta Joshi.

# *One*

## Friday, 16.29

My name's Lizzie McCallum and this is the story of a part of my life: the time when I got mashed up. It wasn't an accident, either. Interested? You should be because it can happen to anyone these days.

I reckon Friday's as good a place to start as any, about twenty-four hours before that smile Patrick gave me. You'll see later why I've got that time on the brain, and probably always will.

Vicky and I were coming out of the Kirkdown swimming baths. I felt fresh and clean, and smelt that way, too – a bit like the kitchen after Mum's given it a wipe round with the bleach. The sun was out, which made it even better. It was one of those comfortable copper late-summer suns, hanging like a kettle in an antique shop.

Vicky spoilt it all, of course, in the way that only your younger sister can. 'Hey, Lizzie,' she called, coming up behind me after she'd gone back to get a chocolate bar from the machine in the foyer, 'what's the matter with your hair?'

Now, I knew there was nothing wrong with my hair. At least, nothing *specially* wrong. It's always crazy after I've been swimming, tying itself into rats' tails like the snakes on the head of that Greek witch woman in the old story. Anyway, that was how my hair was and that was how it would stay until it dried. I knew it even before I looked in the mirror, and the last thing I needed was Vicky reminding me.

I ignored her. I was hoping my hair would dry out before we got to Carson Street. You never knew who you might meet there. It was where those Catholic boys from the Sacred Heart Secondary hung out, like Bobby Devlin and Patrick O'Brien.

Vicky had caught up with me now. 'You deaf or something, Lizzie? I said, what's wrong with your hair?'

I didn't want to get angry with her, she being only eleven and it being such a nice afternoon and all that. 'Just wet, that's all. We've been swimming, if you hadn't noticed.'

I shouldn't have said that. When someone has a go at you, it's best to keep quiet, then you don't get two sides. You can't have an argument or a fight or anything with only one side. That's something I've learned since the killing. Learned the hard way, but not as hard as some, for sure.

Vicky came back at me. 'No need to be all sarky, Lizzie. Just because you're two years older than me, it doesn't mean I can't ask about your hair.' She walked beside me in silence for a few steps then started again. 'I said, what's the problem?'

'Nothing.'

'Then why do you keep trying to see what it looks like in windows?'

'Shut up! I don't.'

'Yes you do. I've been watching.'

That was it. I'd had enough. 'Listen, Vicky – why don't you mind your own business? You know my hair goes all funny when it's wet, so why go on about it, eh?'

'Because I know why you're worried.'

'And what's that supposed to mean?'

'You don't want *someone* to see you with messed-up hair.'

'Listen to you, Little Miss Know-all! So who's this "someone", then?'

'Someone we might see on the way home.'

I love my sister. I haven't got any choice, have I? She's the only one I've got. But she can be that annoying, like a wasp at a picnic. Especially when she tells you things about yourself you didn't know.

'Go on, then,' I said. 'Who's this mystery man?'

'Who said it's a man, Lizzie? It's a boy.'

'You're not thinking of that Tommy Graham, are you? Give me some credit, will you Vicky?'

'Of course it's not Tommy. It's that Patrick O'Brien, isn't it?'

See what I mean? I said Vicky could come up with things you couldn't even have guessed.

'*Patrick O'Brien?* Oh, come off it, Vicky! He's a Catholic, for God's sake! And a wimp! And he's not even good looking. You wouldn't catch me even going down the same side of the street as him. What do you take me for?'

I was surprised at how angry I sounded.

Vicky was, too. 'All right, Lizzie,' she muttered. 'Don't blow a fuse.'

'Then don't you go talking like that. If our dad heard you, he'd go berserk. Think about that, will you?'

She did and she said she was sorry and I said it was nothing. Except it wasn't nothing. Somewhere, hiding at the back of my mind, was a little wee thought that the reason I had flared up so cross was that I wanted to convince myself.

I was never exactly cut out for Hollywood, even before

getting mashed up. My teeth stuck out too far at the front and my bum too far at the back. Judging by what I'd seen of Patrick (which wasn't that much – just a bit of shouting across the street on the way back from school), he wasn't going to be a film star either. But, even at a distance, you could tell he had, well, special eyes. *Irish eyes*, they call them. Bright green and full of mischief.

Ten minutes later, swinging the bags with our wet swimming things in and chatting away about nothing very much, we came round the corner of Carson Street – and there he was.

Patrick O'Brien, sitting with Bobby Devlin on the wall outside number 76. As if they'd been waiting for us. I wanted to turn round and go home the long way down Liverpool Street, but it was too late. The boys had already seen us.

'Hey, Paddy!' called Bobby, loud enough for us to hear. 'It's them McCallum girls come to see us!'

Patrick slid off the wall, saying nothing.

'Lizzie McCallum,' Bobby shouted across the street, 'is it true what they say about you?'

I took Vicky's hand. 'Don't say anything, Vicky. Just keep on walking. They won't dare do anything here, not in daylight.'

I glanced across the street. Now that's what I didn't want, Irish eyes or no Irish eyes: about ten yards ahead of us, the boys had left the pavement and were crossing over to our side.

# *Two*

## Friday, 16.43

When those boys came over the road, for a few seconds I felt I wasn't quite there. It was like watching an old Western: the good guys walking down Main Street, minding their own business but half expecting something, when the doors of the saloon swing open and out come a couple of boozed-up no-goods with chins as stubbly as doormats.

Actually, other than there were four people meeting in the street, it wasn't like that at all. For a start, Patrick and Bobby didn't look as if they were into booze any more than they were into shaving. They were just kids hanging about on a Friday afternoon and, because they were boys, they were looking for a bit of excitement. Something to set the heart thumping, to brag about to their mates at school on Monday. About how they'd got the McCallum girls.

I wasn't frightened. The boys were only my age and not

much bigger than me. Vicky's small, though, and I could feel she was scared by the way her hand went tight in mine. I'd have done anything to stop her getting hurt – funny how that instinct comes out in an emergency.

Bobby stood square in the middle of the pavement, so there was no getting round him without stepping into the road. Patrick was just behind him, his green eyes as wide as CDs.

I went right up to Bobby. When he didn't move, I tried to squeeze by against the hedge of number 73. He moved across to close the gap. His puffed-up jacket, black with some logo on it, made him look bigger than he really was.

'Where you going, then?' he said.

I stepped back and looked slowly – real cool, like film stars do – first at Bobby and then at Patrick. Bobby's eyes were dark, like his jacket, and he had a red spot on the side of his nose. The freckles on Patrick's face looked as if they were under glass, like the patterns on the cups and saucers Mum got free at the supermarket with her points. When I broke one, it exploded into a million shining pieces all over the kitchen.

'Vicky,' I said, sliding my eyes off the boys and looking down at her, 'you noticed the smell around here?' I tried to sound posh and remote, like Mum when she's on the phone to the gas or the electric. 'Wasn't here when we came out earlier, was it now? Must be somebody hasn't cleaned up after their dog.'

Vicky said nothing, just squeezed my hand tighter.

'I said, where you going?' repeated Bobby. He sounded more angry this time.

I was pleased because it meant he hadn't liked what I'd said about him stinking of dog pooh. 'Mind your own business, Bobby Devlin,' I said. 'And get out of my way, please. This is a public footpath and I have a right to go down it.' I'd learned that from the TV, where people are always going on about their 'rights'. It brings God on to their side somehow, or at least the European Union.

'This is a Catholic street,' said Patrick, speaking over Bobby's shoulder. 'Prods aren't welcome here. 'Specially not those with hair like rats' tails.'

That was it. He knew how to get at a girl, that Patrick. I suppose I could have been flattered he'd even noticed my hair, but I just burst. Shouting the worst words I knew, I let go of Vicky's hand and jumped forward like a rugby player. Bobby got half out of the way. I knocked against him, rebounded into the hedge, then bounced out against Patrick. He took a step back and gave me such an odd look – surprise, mostly, but with some fear and I think a wee hint of regret at what he'd said. His mouth moved like the start of the word 'sorry'.

The word didn't come. Instead, there was this car horn going off right beside us. I thought it was the police.

It was worse. It was our dad, coming back from work early. Through the windscreen, I could see his face purple with anger. He stopped the car and leaned across to open the front passenger door.

'Get in!' he shouted. 'Get in the bloody car!'

Vicky jumped in the front. Dad leaned across and unlocked the back door. Just then, Vicky yelled, 'My bag, Lizzie! I've dropped my bag!'

I looked round. The bag with her swimming things in it was lying on the pavement a couple of metres away. I went over and picked it up.

Bobby and Patrick had backed off when our dad showed up. Now, just as I was getting up with Vicky's bag, Patrick stepped up close to me. 'You've got away for now, Lizzie McCallum. But you won't next time – I'll be waiting.'

He spoke so quietly maybe even Bobby hadn't heard. What's more, he sounded like he didn't know what he wanted to say: some of him wanted it to be a threat, but another part of him wanted it to be something else.

So he'd be waiting, I thought. But what for?

## *Three*

# Friday, 17.05

'What the hell was all that about?' asked Dad when we were safe in the car and driving off. I could tell he was still angry because he almost forgot to stop at the traffic lights at the end of Carson Street.

'Nothing,' I said.

'*Nothing?* I don't call my daughter fighting in the street nothing!'

Before I could reply, Vicky said, 'It was Bobby Devlin and Patrick O'Brien, Dad. They started it. They said we couldn't go down the street 'cause it was Catholic and Lizzie said we could . . .'

'Carson Street? *Catholic!* What in the name of God is this place coming to?' Dad often said that – 'what's this place coming to?' – and even more after Uncle Jim had been killed. He didn't expect an answer, of course, because he already knew it. We knew it, too. We'd been told it all our lives – 'this place', our Ulster, was being taken over by the Catholic bandits. Bit by bit. Step by step.

Dad half looked over his shoulder at me. 'Listen here, Lizzie. If I've said it once, I've said it a thousand times: just you stay away from those murdering Fenians. Have you got that, girl?'

'Yes, Dad.'

'I'm not saying it was your fault. Just don't go near them, that's all. Don't get involved.'

'Yes, Dad.'

'Devlin, was it? And O'Brien? I might have guessed. Another generation of Catholic killers on the way . . .'

As Dad went on, I wondered whether Patrick O'Brien really would turn into a killer. It wasn't difficult to work out Bobby Devlin – he was rotten right through, like most Catholics had to be. But Patrick? He knew how to hurt, but that wasn't the same as killing, was it? Sharp tongue did not mean sharp gun. Besides, how could a murderer have green eyes and freckles like that? Dad had often said the devil was a master of disguises and the most dangerous Catholic was a smiling one, so I supposed that was the answer. It made sense, after all, even if it was a bit hard to take.

Dad had cooled off by the time we got back home. I went

out the back to hang our wet swimming things on the line. While I was there, I heard Dad telling Mum about what he'd seen.

'. . . and her being with young Vicky and all,' he finished.

'The O'Brien boy, was it?' said Mum. 'Can't say that's a surprise, knowing what we do of that lot.'

'What do you know, Mum?' I called from the garden. Patrick had got under my skin. I was cross with him for what he had said about my hair, but I was also glad that he had noticed. I suppose I wanted him to have a fair trial.

Mum put her head out of the kitchen window. 'Mrs Renfrew says she heard from her nephew in the Constabulary that it's one of the O'Briens that's top of the list of suspects for who shot your Uncle Jim.' She spoke quietly, as if her words were bombs that might go off if they were thrown about too carelessly. That's the way a lot of things are said in Northern Ireland. We know, like they said on those posters we were shown in history classes, that careless talk costs lives.

'There's no proving it, though?' I said.

'There never is,' said Mum, shutting the window. I finished hanging out the swimming things then went to my room to listen to some music.

Uncle Jim, Mum's brother, had been shot dead last year. Well, he wasn't shot stone dead straight off, if you know what I mean. He was in a bar in Belfast when a gunman came right up to him, fired three shots, then got into a car and disappeared before anyone realized what had happened. Uncle Jim died in hospital later that night.

I read the full story in the paper because Mum and Dad wouldn't talk about it. Still don't much. I was sad, but more for Auntie Jacqui than Uncle Jim. She came to live with us for a couple of weeks afterwards. Every day, when I left to go to school she would sit in the kitchen crying her eyes out, and when I came back she'd still be there, as if she'd never stopped crying all day.

Sadder than that was what she said about Uncle Jim. She said things like he was such a good man and wouldn't hurt a fly. I knew it wasn't true because I'd seen Auntie Jacqui after he'd had a go at her. Long before his murder, Auntie Jacqui had come round a dozen times for a shoulder to cry on and some witch hazel for her bruises.

The paper said Uncle Jim had probably been mistaken for a member of some loyalist paramilitary gang. Or not mistaken . . .

## *Four*

# Friday, 21.00

It's not easy now – since I got mashed up, I mean – to remember exactly how things were then and how I saw them. Because everything's changed, sometimes I get then and now muddled up, especially how I thought about things. I'm doing my best not to invent anything. I want to set it out as it really was, and remember how I really was, too.

We watched TV that Friday evening – some drama, I think, then the news. Mum and Dad always watched the BBC news and made us watch it. Even when I was doing my homework, Mum would call upstairs, 'News, Lizzie! Come down and watch.' She gave me dirty looks if I was late.

It had to be the BBC because the 'B' stood for British. 'Our roots,' Dad explained. The news, he said, linked us to the queen and the flag. Like all our friends, we had a photo of the queen in the living-room. Ours was over the fire, so you saw it as soon as you came in. It was taken about the time Mum and Dad got married and Her Majesty looked a lot younger than she does today. The colours were fading, too. When I asked Dad why he didn't get a new picture, he said it was part of the home, like the front door. You didn't change things like that just for the sake of it.

We had a Union flag folded up behind the towels in the airing cupboard at the top of the stairs. It came out for marches and special occasions. To Mum and Dad it was something religious, that flag – like the cloth that's hung over the altar in some churches. Vicky and I were scared stiff of doing anything disrespectful to it.

Once, after some parade, Dad took it down from the front of the house then got called away before he had put it back in the airing cupboard. Mum was out, too. So this flag stayed there, all spread out over the living-room chairs, making the place look like it had been shut up. Vicky and I watched TV standing by the door. We didn't dare move the flag to sit down.

Anyway, that Friday evening there was this usual stuff on the news about the Good Friday Agreement. Would it last? asked the reporter. Would all the parties accept it? Would the terrorists start handing in their weapons? Same old questions, I thought, round and round.

Mum and Dad had a bit of an argument. It started when the reporter was interviewing some professor who said there was – these were his exact words – 'a real chance for peace in Northern Ireland'.

Dad swore, real strong. Mum said he shouldn't talk like that in front of the children.

Dad said she shouldn't be so fussy. 'It's no worse than they hear every day at school, Janice. Besides, it's true.'

'What is?' asked Mum.

'This agreement hasn't got a chance. No Catholic's ever stuck to what's written on a piece of paper in his life before, so why should he start now? Tell me that now, Janice.'

Mum said she thought this time might be different.

'Maybe shooting Jim was different,' said Dad. He was sitting up in his chair, straight as a gate post.

'Don't bring Jim into it,' said Mum. I could see she was getting upset, too. She had pink patches on her cheeks, like make-up for a play.

'Why not? He was my brother-in-law, wasn't he? Did he deserve to die?'

'Don't be silly, Michael. Anyway, you knew more than me about what he got up to.'

'What he got up to? What's that supposed to mean, Janice?'

Before Mum could tell him, Vicky started crying. I told

her to shut up so I could watch the news. I didn't want to, of course. I just wanted Mum and Dad to stop.

Vicky's crying did it and we watched up to the weather in silence. The bloke in glasses smiled and said it would be a nice day in Northern Ireland tomorrow. He showed us bright green under a fake sun. Then he told us to make the most of it because it wouldn't last. He stood back and showed us loads of black lines off to the left. They were coming our way, he said, and it wouldn't be much fun. End of the summer.

In a way, he was right.

When I went to bed, Mum and Dad said they were sorry for arguing. 'It's just difficult at the moment, Lizzie, what with everyone hoping but no one sure,' said Dad.

'Don't worry,' I said.

'Don't you worry, either,' said Mum. 'You've got everything to live for.'

I liked the sound of that. 'You think so?' I asked.

'For sure,' said Mum. 'You're the future, Lizzie. You, Vicky – all the young. You've got everything to live for.'

I smiled.

'But don't go spoiling it by messing with those kids in Carson Street,' said Dad. He always had to get the last word in.

'I wasn't messing . . .'

'I know, I know,' said Dad. 'I wasn't your fault. Just be careful, that's all, because—'

'I've got everything to live for,' I finished, chiming the words like a poem.

Mum and Dad laughed. I was still grinning when I went into the bathroom to clean my teeth.

## *Five*

# Saturday, 09.21

The man on the TV was right. The sun was shining when I woke up and by the time I came down to breakfast it was already quite warm. Dad was outside fixing something on the car. Mum was pulling things out of the washing machine and shoving them into a plastic basket.

'Afternoon,' she said when I came into the kitchen.

I ignored the remark. 'Morning, Mum,' I said. I opened the cupboard near the fridge and helped myself to a bowl of cereal. 'Where's Vicky?'

'Round Tracy's. Why?'

'I need to go into town this morning. Thought she'd like to come.'

'It'd help me. I might even trust you to get her school shoes.' She gave me a funny look, as if she'd just remembered something, and added, 'But why're you so keen to get out, Lizzie, after that trouble yesterday and all?'

I knew she'd ask. What I really wanted was to buy postcards to stick in the holiday diary I was keeping for school, but I didn't want to tell Mum. I was ten or eleven days behind with my diary and planned to catch up on Sunday, after I'd got the postcards. If she found out how far behind I was, she'd make me stay in all morning and get it up to date, postcards or no postcards. Then I wouldn't be able to go down town until the afternoon. I didn't want that because everyone would be there then, people like Bobby Devlin and Patrick O'Brien.

I'd thought a lot about Friday – about the boys hassling us in Carson Street, Patrick saying he'd be waiting and so on. Those eyes of his were like magnets, so part of me couldn't help wanting to go back and see what would happen, good or bad. But I'd also thought about what Mum and Dad had said. As Uncle Jim discovered, you couldn't mix chasing Catholics and having everything to live for.

I'd decided not to find out why Patrick O'Brien would be waiting. Instead, I'd go into town in the morning, when he'd be playing football, and go the long way round, down Liverpool Street, just to be sure.

That was my plan. I sometimes think how different things would have been if I'd been able to stick to it.

It was Mum that messed it up, though it was my fault.

I said I needed to get felt pens for school. That was daft, wasn't it? The minute she heard the words 'pen' and 'school', Mum's mind switched to questioning mode.

'So how's the diary going, Lizzie?' she asked. 'Haven't seen you at it much lately. Thought you wanted to win the class prize?'

'OK thanks, Mum. Going well. Yeah, I do want the prize.'

She gave me a strange look. 'Is that so, Lizzie? Well, if you'd like to bring it down here into the kitchen, maybe we could go over it together. I might be able to help, you know.'

It was a private diary, I said. Anyway, I'd lost the argument. That sort of thing doesn't wash with our mum. Down I came with the diary, she saw it was almost two weeks behind and that was it: prison. I was sent to my room and told not to come down until the diary was up to date.

'And no skimping!' Mum shouted after me as I stomped back upstairs. 'Half a page for each day, at the very least!'

So that was all the morning gone.

I don't reckon anyone could sit in a bedroom and write a diary flat out for more than about half an hour. Not even Shakespeare. I wasn't in his league, so I managed about ten minutes before my mind started drifting off.

You can guess what I thought about, can't you? If I went into town in the afternoon, I was bound to see him. All the lads, Catholic and Protestant, hung about the High Street on Saturday afternoons. There wasn't much trouble normally because they kept themselves to themselves. Sometimes there was a bit of shouting and throwing things, but not much. Nothing like in Belfast or Portadown or one of those other places with barbed wire and bricked-up windows.

So what if Patrick saw me? I thought. He couldn't do any harm, not there in the High Street. OK, I decided, I'd go. I'd be just as safe there as staying back home.

To make myself feel stronger, I tore a page from the back of my diary and drew a picture of Patrick on it. Then I stuck my pen through each of those big green eyes. I'm really ashamed of it now. I'd like to wind that part of my life back, like a video, and re-run it. To tell you the truth, I felt bad even when I was stabbing, so I whispered what Dad had said, 'The most dangerous Catholic is a smiling one.'

Uncle Jim used to go further than that. He talked about the Bible, about how there was no Pope in it, so the Pope must have come from the devil. 'Antichrist', he called him. Pure evil.

I didn't know about that. But I did know about the

murders and things that had been going on since before I was born, and how it was always the Catholics that started it. That meant, even if they weren't pure evil, they had a load of it in them.

At least, that's how I worked it out then. Before the killing.

## *Six*

# Saturday, 13.45

At last I finished my diary. I have to admit, it looked great. I left gaps for the postcards and wrote some good stuff in between.

You know what diaries can be like, just a boring list of 'got up', 'had breakfast', and so on. Well, our English teacher, Mrs McCaskell, the one who organized the diary competition, she told us not to write like that. She said she wanted a diary that 'hummed'. It was a funny word to use, 'hummed', but I knew what she meant. She wanted us to describe things and say how we felt about them, make our diaries hum with life.

I didn't put down anything private. I didn't want anyone, not even Mrs McCaskell, reading about that. But I did write some good descriptions, like of the day we went to Loch Neagh and Dad fell in the water because he was showing off to Vicky and me (and maybe also to Mum).

That was a fun day, that was – the sort you remember when things go wrong later.

Mum didn't even check my diary. She trusted me, which made me forgive her for making me stay in all morning. She just asked how it had gone and I said 'great' and that was it. She knew I liked writing. When I started secondary school, Dad asked if I wanted to be a journalist. I said I might. I still might, but not in Northern Ireland.

'I've seen a pair of shoes in Arnold's that are £17.99,' said Mum. Dad was doing the washing up. It was his Saturday job. He complained like mad when Mum first suggested it, but she said he had to if he wanted to be a new man. Of course, he said he was happy being an old man but it didn't make any difference. By now he'd even begun to enjoy it.

'That's a good price, Mum,' I said. 'You sure they'll last?'

'I don't want 'em to last,' said Vicky. 'I want 'em to look good.'

I came over all older sister and told her to think of Mum and Dad and how they weren't made of money.

'Can't say you were thinking of Mum and Dad when you got your trainers,' said Vicky. My sister was sharp for only eleven.

‘That was different,’ I said. ‘They weren’t for school.’

‘So what?’ said Vicky.

Mum interrupted. ‘You’ll see them in the window, Lizzie. On the left. There’s a big display with a notice about going back to school. They’re on special offer.’

‘No problem, Mum,’ I said. ‘What size are you, Vicky?’

‘Three.’

‘That was last time,’ said Mum. ‘You’d better get them to measure her, Lizzie. Don’t get them too small, whatever you do. I can’t afford another pair before Christmas.’ She went over to the worktop beside the sink and picked up her bag. ‘Here, I’ve only got two tenners, so make sure you don’t lose them. Two pounds and a penny change.’

‘Can we use it for the bus?’ I asked.

‘On the way back,’ said Mum. ‘They won’t give you change for a tenner on the way in.’

I took the money and stuffed it into the side pocket of my jeans. As I did so, I felt a flutter of worry. It was a lot of money to be carrying about. ‘Don’t suppose there’s a chance of a lift, is there, Dad?’ I asked.

Dad looked up from the sink. He’d put too much washing-up liquid in the bowl and the foam was up to his elbows. ‘If you wait a couple of hours, Lizzie. I’m putting on new brake shoes and I’ve got the wheels off the back of the car. Won’t get far on only two wheels – it’s a *Raleigh* good car, you know, not a *Raleigh* bicycle.'

I groaned, but not in an unkind sort of way. I loved Dad's jokes, even the bad ones. It was the way he came out with them when you weren't expecting it.

Mum was looking at me. 'You're not worried are you, Lizzie?' she said. 'I mean, after yesterday? D'you want me to come with you?'

I could have said yes. Part of me wanted to. If I had . . .

These 'ifs' are beginning to annoy me. They're all about the past, what's gone and finished. That's been the problem with everyone in Northern Ireland, going about with one eye on 'is' and the other on 'was'. It's like trying to drive a car by only looking in the rear-view mirror. You don't get anywhere.

So I said I didn't want Mum to come and there wouldn't be any trouble. Vicky agreed – I think she thought I'd be more likely to get her the sort of shoes she wanted.

We went out just after two. I was in my jeans and new trainers with a blue top I'd bought at Loch Neagh. Vicky was dressed the same, except that she had on a pink top with some tennis logo on it. She was good at sport and said she wanted to be a tennis star when she grew up. Silly, really, because she'd never even played tennis.

## *Seven*

# Saturday, 14.05

As I planned, we took the long way into town, past the supermarket, down Liverpool Street and left into Kimberley Street by the library. We saw nobody, apart from Mr Alder walking that ugly dog of his.

Vicky and I chatted about bands and that sort of stuff, but I was only half concentrating. I felt odd walking along with my right hand stuffed in my jeans' pocket. The money was there, you see, and I was scared it might fall out. I was also wondering whether we'd get away without meeting Bobby and Patrick again.

They weren't outside the library, where they sometimes hung out. They weren't on the corner of Kimberley Street and the High Street, either. A good sign, I thought. Perhaps they hadn't come into town after all.

But they had. We went into Kenny's to see if they had the felt pens and postcards I wanted. When we came out, there they were: Bobby Devlin, Patrick O'Brien and a couple of other boys I didn't know. Patrick was wearing a green top that matched his eyes. They were as bright as ever, despite my voodoo stabbing. I was pleased about that.

'Got your dad to come and rescue you this time, have you?' said Bobby.

Like the day before, I took Vicky's hand. I was determined not to get involved, whatever happened.

'Mind your own business, Bobby Devlin,' I said. 'You and your stupid friends. Now, if you'll get out of our way, Vicky and I have got some shopping to do.' Without looking at anyone in particular and pulling Vicky with me, I pushed through them to the edge of the pavement.

'Who're you calling stupid?' asked a voice behind me. It was Patrick. If it had been one of the others, I wouldn't have replied.

'You,' I said, turning round and looking at him, 'for getting mixed up with the likes of Devlin.'

Patrick opened his mouth, like he'd done yesterday afternoon when I thought he was going to say sorry. Again, he didn't say anything. He did something much worse, though. So surprising I'll never forget it as long as I live.

He winked at me.

It was unreal. I glanced down at Vicky to see if she'd noticed but she was staring at the ground. When I looked back at Patrick, he had turned round and was talking to his friends.

I needed to get away. 'Come on, Vicky! Let's go and get your shoes,' I said. I checked there was no traffic, crossed to the other side of the street and set off towards Arnold's.

As we crossed, Vicky said something about hoping they weren't following us. I wasn't really listening because I was all confused. Who'd have thought that something as small and simple as a wink could do that? It wasn't right. It wasn't fair, either. I had been so determined to hate him, or at least have nothing to do with him . . . and now I found myself wanting to look round, to see where he was.

Vicky did it for me, speaking twice before I heard her. 'Lizzie, I said they're following us!'

I turned my head. The boys had crossed the High Street and were coming up behind us. 'Doesn't matter,' I said. 'Don't take any notice. They'll soon get bored. Little things amuse little minds.' Little things like winks, I thought.

'Shouldn't we cross over again?' Vicky asked.

'What's the point? We'll only have to come back again.'

'I don't like it, Lizzie,' said Vicky. 'I wish I'd never come.' I could hear the tears in her voice. I had to think fast. What did Mum do when Vicky started playing up? She distracted her.

'Here,' I said, 'd'you want some chewing gum?'

'Sure, Lizzie! Have you got some money then?'

'Just a bit. Let's go!' We went into the newsagent's next to the butcher's. It was dark inside and smelt of tobacco and papers. I bought Vicky a packet of sugar-free, which she liked best.

After I'd paid, I told Vicky to stay where she was and went to the door to see where the boys were. They were all crowded round the TV rental shop two doors down, watching some sport through the window. Vicky and I were out and over the street before they even looked up.

I was glad for Vicky's sake but not for mine. I wanted to check out that wink. Had I imagined it? Was it some kind of twitch, or was it real? I imagined Dad warning me, 'Remember, Lizzie, the most dangerous Catholic is a winking one.'

'What're you smiling at?' said Vicky. I hadn't noticed her looking at me.

'Just something I was thinking.'

'What?'

'Mind your own business.'

'It's not that Patrick O'Brien again, is it?'

'Of course it isn't!'

Of course it was. We were almost outside Arnold's now but on the wrong side of the road. I stopped and looked to see if there were any cars coming. Out of the corner of my eye I noticed the boys further down the street. They were on the edge of the pavement, looking for us.

Patrick saw us first and turned to tell his friends. At the same moment, I heard the siren in the distance.

## *Eight*

## Saturday, 14.32

I expect you think I'm going to say that the siren struck terror into my heart, or something like that. Wrong. To tell the truth, I didn't take much notice of it. It was coming from somewhere over the other side of town. The only reason I remember hearing it was that it started at the same time as Patrick saw us.

Staying on their side of the street, the boys were walking up to where we were. Vicky and I saw them coming and decided to get over to Arnold's straight away. We never got there. In fact, we never even got off the pavement.

The siren was louder now, so everyone could hear it. I wondered whether it was the police or an ambulance. I hoped it wasn't an ambulance because that meant someone was seriously ill or there'd been an accident.

It was the police. Two cars came in from Armagh Road,

revving and roaring right up to where we were standing, then squealing and stopping like American TV cops. A third soon came up behind. The sirens cut out when they stopped, but not the lights. They went on like a daylight disco – flash, flash, flash – while the police jumped out and started shouting to us through megaphones. 'This is an emergency. Do not panic. Move in an orderly fashion to the other end of the High Street. Keep calm. Please move in an orderly fashion . . .'

All the time, the radios in the police cars were still going. One car was just in front of us. The voice on the radio was going on about 'location' and 'code word'. Though he didn't say the word 'bomb', I guessed that was what it was all about.

'Keep calm. Please move in an orderly fashion . . .'

There was no need to tell us that. We'd heard it all before. Everyone in Northern Ireland was used to bomb scares. We'd even had them in our little town. Our primary school had six in one term. Vicky and I knew what to do and how long it all took. Just as we knew that bomb scares were only that – scares.

'D'you think it's a bomb, Lizzie?' Vicky asked. We had started moving the way the police told us.

'Most likely,' I said. 'A scare.'

A man with a beard and wearing a yellow anorak pushed

past us. He looked as if he'd come out of a fishfinger advert. 'Supposed to be a bloody cease-fire!' he muttered.

I thought of what Dad had said the night before about the Agreement not working and reckoned he and the fishfinger advert man ought to get together for a good moan.

'What about my shoes?' said Vicky.

I put my arm round her shoulders and gave her a hug. 'Don't worry, Vicky,' I said. 'There's another week before school starts.'

'You mean we won't be able to get them today?' Vicky asked.

'I think we'd better go home,' I said. 'This'll go on for ages.'

We were part of a small crowd now – men, women, children, babies in pushchairs, old people with sticks, shop assistants in their uniforms – all walking down the street. I remember thinking we were like the children in the Pied Piper poem that Mrs McCaskell had read to us, except there wasn't a piper.

As we walked, I looked out for the boys on the other side of the road. I couldn't see them. People began spilling off the pavements into the street. The traffic had been stopped, so I did the same, taking Vicky with me. It made sense because there was more room and I thought maybe I could see where the boys had got to. I didn't want Bobby Devlin and his mates bumping into us in this crowd, not with me having £20 in my pocket.

That was what I was worried about most, losing that money.

## *Nine*

# Saturday, 14.37

I think what made the killing so bad was that everything was so normal beforehand. You can imagine how relaxed it all was: Saturday afternoon, half the town out shopping or meeting for a chat, sun shining, summer holidays . . .

Even with the police shouting and us walking like refugees down the High Street, it wasn't really frightening. After all, both sides had signed a peace agreement, hadn't they?

While I was still looking for the boys, I felt this push in my back. I shoved my hand down my pocket to keep the tenners safe and looked round. It was Emily Wright and her friend Sam Lochy from school. I was glad to see them.

'Hi, Lizzie!' said Emily. 'What're you doing, then?'

'Same as you,' I said. 'Doing what the police say. Just walking.'

Emily made a clicking noise with her tongue. 'Don't be silly, Lizzie. I mean what're you doing in town? Shopping?'

I nodded. 'Vicky's school shoes.'

'But I won't be getting them now,' said Vicky. 'I hate these stupid bomb scares.'

Sam had long fair hair tied back with a purple band. Her face was round and kind. 'So do I, Vicky,' she said. 'I'm going abroad when I'm older. Get away from all this rubbish.'

On my left I noticed our neighbour, Mr Kilshaw, from number 16. He had a carrier bag in each hand, bulging with the shape of beer cans. 'Afternoon, Mr Kilshaw!' I said. 'Been shopping?'

He turned and smiled. Hurrying along the High Street, which had a slope on it, had made his face all sweaty. 'Afternoon, Lizzie! And you, little Vicky! Isn't this just a fine pain in the backside?'

'Sure,' I said. It was, too. A real pain in the backside.

Emily and Sam fell back a bit. I kept a tight hold of Vicky's hand and looked for the boys again. Up ahead there was a red car parked on the other side of the road. The crowd was splitting and flowing round it like a river round an island. One or two of them were so close they brushed along its sides. I wondered whether their zips and rings were scratching it, and what the owner would say when he came back and saw what had happened.

Funny that I thought that, isn't it? It was the wrong way round: people damaging the car not the car damaging people, which is what happened. 'Damaged' is not the right word, though; it's too soft. Damage can usually be repaired. Most of what happened to people that Saturday afternoon can never be repaired. Ever.

I was glad when I saw Bobby's black jacket because by then he was level with the car and legging it up the street away from us. His two friends were just behind him. But there was no sign of Patrick. I went a bit further into the road, looking for that green sweatshirt of his.

I didn't see him at first because I was looking too far. He'd left his mates and was walking almost level with Vicky and me, only a few metres away on the other side of the road. When I spotted him he was staring straight at me.

I stared back. He gave a sort of grin, like he was embarrassed or something, then looked away. What am I doing? I thought. Here's the guy you were sticking your pen into, the guy you said you'd have nothing to do with. What's got into you, girl?

I waited for Patrick to look up again. Without realizing it, I was drifting towards the middle of the road. Vicky pulled me back. 'Can't you walk straight, Lizzie?' she said. 'Come on!'

I ended up right at the edge of the kerb, in the gutter. Vicky was to my right, on the pavement. 'That's better! I'm the same height as you now, Lizzie,' she said.

'So you are!' I said. 'You've grown real quick!'

'Don't be silly,' she said.

I glanced back across the road. Patrick was ahead of me now, just level with the red car. When he reached it, he turned round and looked for me. And do you know what that no-good Catholic did when he saw me?

He smiled – the biggest and friendliest smile I'd seen in ages.

## *Ten*

# Saturday, 14.40

Nobody talked about it afterwards. They were being kind, of course – they thought I didn't want to talk about it. They were right, at first, because I really did want to forget everything. I hoped I'd wake up and find I'd been dreaming. I wanted to take the part of my brain which had it stored and scrape it clean. Press the 'erase' button.

But it's not so easy. You can't scrape the inside of a brain. It's like a computer: when a PC crashes and everything on it's lost, there are these experts who can bring it all back. Once you've got stuff on your hard disc, you can't wipe it right off. Not completely. There's always what they call an 'impression' left. It's the same with our memories. Once something's gone in, it's there for ever. Maybe even after we're dead. So when I tried to forget about the bomb, I was just avoiding it. It was lurking there all the time, just as it had been in that red car.

Mrs O'Reilly explained this to me. She was my counsellor and she said that one day, when I was ready, she'd like me to try and open all the cupboard doors in my memory and look inside. If I did that, she said, there'd probably be no more ghosts. I did it, in the end, but only when she was there to help me.

When I first looked, lots of the cupboards were empty. The one the explosion was supposed to be in was just space, what they call a black hole. Mrs O'Reilly said this was normal – the mind doesn't register what she called 'major trauma'. It switches off to stop the fuses blowing.

I'm not sure that this is true. The trouble is, what I remember and what I've read since have become muddled up. But I think it was something like this . . .

There was Patrick, walking round the back of the parked car, looking round at me with that smile on his face – other people around him – me and Vicky about thirty metres away on the other side of the road – Vicky up on the pavement, like I've explained, so I was between her and the car – lots of people around us, too – the police still giving orders at the bottom of the High Street, sending people away from them, towards the car.

Towards that car. Towards the bomb. The car bomb.

Somewhere, at the back of one of those cupboards Mrs O'Reilly talks about, I found this picture of the car swelling, like a balloon being filled with air. Blown up, if you want.

The inside filled with an orange flame. The doors bulged and came off. The glass in the windows went all fuzzy then disappeared into a sort of rain. The people nearest the car started flying. I like to think of them as souls, starting on their way to heaven.

There must have been a noise, although I don't really remember it. But I do remember the blast.

Like a concrete wall it came. It took Vicky's hand clean out of mine, picked me up, knocked me over, threw me down – I don't know, I really don't know. Just a rush, then silence and darkness and nothingness.

Like going to sleep.

## *Eleven*

# Saturday, 14.43

When you've been unconscious, like I was, your hearing comes back first. Before you see or smell or taste or feel. Yes, long before you feel, thank God.

Noises. Someone screaming, another groaning. No, not one or two people, lots of them. The whole crowd that had been in the High Street, all of them in a chorus of every unhappy sound you can imagine. And in the background were alarm bells, set off by the blast.

I lay there listening but not taking it in. Time went by as slowly as a sail boat. I don't suppose it was more than a minute or two, but for all I knew it could have been a week, a month, a millennium.

After a while, one sound was blotting out the others. It was a sort of gasping or gurgling coming from somewhere near my head. My eyes refused to open, so I tried to feel what it was with my hand.

I was lying with my right arm underneath me and didn't want to move to get it out. I tried the other side. Very slowly, I lifted my left hand and moved it towards the noise. My fingers found this soft, squashy thing. I knew what it was meant to be because it had an ear and a sort of nose-shape in the middle. But it didn't feel right. It shouldn't have been so wet and sticky.

I opened my eyes and looked. It was a woman, her head just six inches away from mine. I saw what I had been feeling – it wasn't a face any more, just a bloody mess. Out of the middle of it came the sound I had heard, her breathing.

I tried to scream. No sound came out. I shut my eyes. The woman made a strange noise, like the last bath water going down the plug hole, then was quiet.

Oh, dear God, I thought, I must be dead. I opened my eyes again. No, this wasn't death, this was still part of Lizzie McCallum's life.

Gradually, it started to come back to me. The crowd, the car, the explosion. Far away, I heard sirens. Then the pain began, somewhere below my waist. It was just a throb at first but it grew and grew every second until it hurt so much I tried to scream again. This time a thin cry came out, like a bird high up on a windy day.

Through the pain came the worry. There were things I had to do. I rolled over so my right arm was free. It hurt but at least I could move it. Very slowly, I lifted my head and shoulders and looked around.

I couldn't take in what I saw. I still can't, even after all the help Mrs O'Reilly's given me. The bomb had laid this multi-coloured carpet of bodies and glass and things I couldn't make out all over the High Street. What I remember most was the blood. I never knew people had so much blood in them.

The sight made the worry worse, but before I could focus on it the pain returned. This time I knew it was my leg, my left leg. I looked down . . .

Oh, no! That can't be me, I thought. It's not real. Things like that don't happen here, only in the news from places like Belfast and Bosnia.

I looked away and screamed again. This time I made more noise, but the effort exhausted me. I put my head back on the road and closed my eyes.

'Can you hear me, dearie? Can you hear me?' Because the voice was coming from right next to me, I thought it was the woman with the bashed-in face.

'No!' I said. 'Leave me alone!'

I felt a hand on my arm. 'It's all right, dearie. Take it easy now.' I realized it was a man's voice. 'We'll soon be getting you some help.' He called out something, a name I think. Then a woman was asking me about my leg and saying how she was going to put something round it to stop the bleeding.

I didn't care about the bleeding. I just wanted it to stop hurting and be better again. I didn't want it to stay a mess like that. I didn't want crutches or a wheelchair.

Gentle hands took hold of my jeans to raise my leg. The movement reminded me. 'Mum's money,' I muttered. 'Don't take it!'

Then I remembered why the money was there – what I'd been worried about all along. I panicked and tried to sit up. 'Vicky! Where's Vicky?' I said. I sounded like I was about six again.

'I'm sure Vicky's OK,' said the woman. 'Now just lie down and relax.'

The pain was getting worse now – not coming in waves but there all the time. It sank its teeth into my leg so that it hurt and hurt and hurt . . .

When the woman had finished, she knelt beside me and stroked my forehead. 'What's your name, love?' she asked.

I tried to say 'Lizzie' but it just came out as crying. I opened my eyes. The woman had turned away and was waving at someone. 'Quick!' she said. When she looked back at me and saw my eyes were open, she smiled. But it was too late. I'd already seen the truth in her face.

She pitied me.

## *Twelve*

# Saturday, 15.29

I started shaking when I saw the woman's look. It was the shock of everything catching up with me, I reckon. I was crying, too – not howling like you'd expect but whimpering, like a dog or a baby. I wanted it to stop hurting, I wanted Vicky, I wanted my mum, I wanted to tell her the two tenners were safe . . .

The next thing I remember is the woman talking to me again. Do you know, I never knew her name? She just floated into my world, cared for me, then floated out again. Sometimes I think she wasn't a person at all but my guardian angel. Everyone's supposed to have one, a spirit that turns up when you need them most. I needed mine then, for sure.

'We're going to move you now, Lizzie,' she said, still stroking my head. 'You're going to hospital.'

I tried to fix my eyes on her but they kept closing or

clouding over. 'How d'you know my name?' I asked. I was still shaking and sobbing.

She smiled again. 'Your sister Vicky told us. She's safe. Your mum and dad are on their way to get her.'

I wanted to ask why Mum and Dad weren't coming to get me, but by then I was being lifted up and carried down the High Street towards where the police cars had been. I think about six people must have helped because I felt their hands making a sort of stretcher for me to lie on. They wrapped a blanket round my legs so the left one stayed straight, then lifted me to their shoulders, like a coffin.

My guardian angel walked alongside, talking to me all the time. Her voice was silk soft and cool. 'Almost there, Lizzie. I'm afraid all the ambulances are busy, but they've got you a taxi.'

A taxi? That'll cost us, I thought. In our family it was the car, the bus or walking, almost never a taxi. The last time I'd been in one was after Uncle Jim's funeral, when Dad had drunk too much whiskey to drive home.

I think someone gave me an injection before they laid me across the back seat of the taxi. My guardian angel got in the front, beside the driver. She said something about the blood spoiling the inside of his car.

He swore and said he didn't care. He'd fill it to the roof with blood if it would help. That's what emergencies do to people – bring out the best in them. 'Soon have you there, Lizzie,' he said. 'And there's no need to worry yourself about the fare. I've turned off the meter.' It was his little joke, you see, the sort of thing men say when they're embarrassed or can't think of the right words.

As soon as the door was shut, the taxi driver leaned on his horn and went off like he was in a grand prix. I banged into the back of the seat, then rolled forward. Oh, God! It hurt! I let out a little scream. My angel turned round and put her hand out to steady me.

'Could you go a bit more carefully, Mr Abercrombie?' she said. 'It won't be doing her any good getting thrown around like that.'

'I'm doing my best,' he said, but he didn't slow down much. I think he was frightened I'd die before he got me to the hospital.

After I'd banged about some more, my angel climbed into the back and put her arms round me to stop me falling on to the floor. 'Soon be there, Lizzie,' she said. 'Soon be there.'

I'd been to our hospital twice before. The first time was when Vicky had to have an X-ray on her arm because they thought she'd broken it when she fell over playing football with the boys in the playground. The teachers let me go with her to keep her company. Her arm was only badly bruised. The second time I went with our mum to have what she called a 'check up'. I waited outside the room while they did whatever they needed to do. Later, they sent a letter to say that Mum was negative, which pleased her and Dad a lot.

I liked the hospital those first two times. It had these long, clean corridors that went on for miles. I wanted to have a go down them on my roller blades. While I was waiting for Mum, this nurse came up to me and started chatting. I asked her what all her badges were for. She told me all their names. One of them was for special intensive care training.

I didn't see that nurse the third time I went to the hospital because there wasn't any room for me in intensive care. All the beds were full. The place where Vicky had been for her X-ray was full, too. Even those long corridors and the car parks were full. Believe me, it was chaos. People who knew said it was like a war.

Mr Abercrombie stopped behind an ambulance. Everyone had to wait their turn and I couldn't get into the hospital until the casualties had been taken out of the ambulance. Lying on the back seat of the taxi, all I could see were these lights flashing out of sync – blue, blue, orange, blue, orange, blue, blue, blue, orange . . .

They got me out of the car by putting half a stretcher underneath me, then moving me over and locking in the other half. When they lifted me up, there was a noise like a plaster coming off where my back had stuck to the seat with blood. I felt very weak and kept my eyes closed because the lights were so bright.

Somewhere between getting out of Mr Abercrombie's taxi and going into the hospital, my guardian angel vanished. I feel very bad that I hadn't even said thank you to her.

Men in blue uniforms put me on a bed with wheels and covered me with more blankets. I wanted to go to sleep but a nurse kept waking me up with questions. Name? Age? I didn't know. I didn't care, either.

A second nurse, who pronounced my name 'Leezee', gave me another injection. Then she said something about 'dreep'. I was scared and tried to say no. She didn't take any notice. Instead, she stuck a great big needle in my arm with a tube that went up to a bulgy plastic bag that looked like it should have had sweets in it. Instead, it was full of watery stuff. Then she did the same with my other arm. This time the bag was purple-red, ketchup colour. It was about this time that I stopped hurting so much, but I was still scared.

I was seen by an English doctor who wore metal glasses and a serious expression. She was younger than my mum but she didn't smile. First, she told the nurses to take off the blankets and cut off most of my clothes so she could examine me. She looked at my left leg for ages, muttering medical words to a nurse with grey hair. When she'd finished, she said 'Good luck, Lizzie!' then went on to someone else.

The nurse with grey hair, I think she was a sister, said, 'The doctor says it's best if you're transferred. We'll get you ready.' I didn't have a clue what she was on about.

Two nurses gave me a quick clean up and stuck loads of dressings and bandages on me. I couldn't see properly, but I think they put some sort of plastic bag round my left leg. When they'd finished, and covered me up with clean blankets, one of them said, 'Sorry it's such a mess, Lizzie. Only temporary, just to hold you together till you get there. They'll sort you out properly at the other end.'

The sister came back with a clipboard. She put it on my bed, somewhere near my feet, then nodded. Two men wheeled me through crowds of people and out of the back of the hospital. The road outside was bumpy and my drip bags, red and white, waved like plastic flags.

The air was cool. There was a lot of noise overhead and a great wind, but I wasn't scared any more. I was too far gone to bother about what was going on.

## *Thirteen*

# Saturday, 15.43

The noise was a helicopter. Our hospital couldn't handle all the casualties and the army had been called in to fly patients to emergency departments all over the province. I was one of those who needed to be operated on right away, so I got priority. Front of the queue, first helicopter to land.

It came down on a special pad, next to the car park. We were waiting, five of us I think, lined up and ready to go. I had a nurse with me. Before we got in the helicopter, she told me her name was Kate. Just Kate, no surname or anything. That was a good thing to do because it set up a sort of bond between us, like the beginning of a friendship. I tried to tell her that I was Lizzie, but my mouth wouldn't move. It didn't matter, though, because she knew already.

'Don't you try to talk, Lizzie,' she said. 'Just rest. It'll help you feel better. Promise.'

She smiled down at me and bent forward to give me a

kiss on my forehead. That was such a kind thing to do. I smiled back at her with my eyes and hoped she noticed.

All this time, I was lying on my back, looking up. There were blocks to stop me rolling my head. When I opened my eyes, it was like looking through a viewfinder: all I could see was afternoon sky and bits of tree and the tops of people walking by.

As they were wheeling me towards the helicopter, there was a noise behind me. A man was shouting, 'Stop!' over and over. I knew the voice.

The next minute, Dad's face came into my viewfinder. It was red and twisted. He was crying and his shoulders were going up and down as if he couldn't breathe. It was impossible! My dad didn't cry. He'd never cried before in his life, not even when Uncle Jim was killed.

At first, leaning over my bed, all he could say was 'Lizzie!' Then he said he loved me and would never forgive them for what they'd done to me. I didn't know what he was going on about.

At that time I didn't know what else had happened to me, other than they'd stuck on all those dressings. But Dad could see my face and my hands. Later, when we counted them up, there were thirty-four stitches just in my head. We never bothered to count the rest.

Kate put her hand on my dad's arm and spoke to him.

He looked at me, then kissed me like he hadn't done since I was little. After that, his face slipped out of my viewfinder and I was wheeled into the helicopter.

I'd never been in a helicopter before, but I'd seen loads of army ones flying over the town. Dad sometimes gave a thumbs-up sign when he saw them. 'Just to let them know they're wanted,' he explained.

The inside was dark and smelled of men and oil and equipment. I was lifted off my hospital bed and put on a special army one. It had dark green straps, the same colour as the helicopter, to stop me falling out. The blankets were dark green, too, so were the poles that held up my drips. The army's like that – they like all their stuff to be the same. I suppose it means you can spot it a mile off and it stops people nicking it. Not that I've ever heard of anyone trying to nick a helicopter.

I was against one of the sides of the helicopter. Kate sat next to me and held my hand. There was a lot of noise when we took off but it got better when we were flying. Even so, I couldn't hear much. A couple of soldiers were chatting somewhere near. I think they were talking about the bomb because every other word was 'bastards', or worse. They shut up when Kate said something to them. After that, I can't remember any more. I must have gone to sleep.

## *Fourteen*

# Saturday, 16.37

I think it was still afternoon when the helicopter landed. The truth is, I didn't really know what was going on then, and I know less now. Bits of memory come and go like music on a radio when it's not properly tuned in – clear one minute, all fuzzy the next. I do remember the soldiers, though. When I was taken out of the helicopter they said goodbye and good luck. Their accents were strange – they didn't speak like anywhere in Ireland or on Dad's BBC news. I think they must have been Scottish.

Kate said something about them being good lads. She also told me where we were, but it didn't register. This hospital was bigger than the last one, quieter too. There weren't those doctors, nurses, porters and the like all rushing about, just a few nurses by the door who spoke to Kate and then took me in and wheeled me behind some green curtains. I felt very hot.

A young doctor came in and looked at my clipboard. He said he needed X-rays. That meant another journey: more bright corridors, heavy doors, shoved to this side and that while they took pictures, then the corridors again and back to where I started.

Kate didn't leave me, except when they were taking pictures. I asked her to stay with me because I was frightened again. Very. She said she couldn't stay in the X-ray room because the radiation was dangerous, but she wouldn't go far. I suppose I should have asked why the radiation was dangerous for her but not for me, but I didn't. My brain was too dozey.

The doctor took my X-rays out of a yellow packet and shuffled them through his hands, like holiday snaps, picking out the ones he wanted. A second doctor came in and had a look. They had a chat, then asked a nurse something. She went out and came back with a third doctor.

You know how it is when someone special comes into a room? Well, it was like that when this man came in. He wasn't tall or handsome, just a normal-looking man with grey hair and glasses. But he walked and talked like he knew where he was going and what he was doing – a no-nonsense, listen-to-me person, like a headteacher. Everyone straightened up a bit, like they knew something was going to happen. I felt the same. Even though he hadn't done anything yet, I knew he would and it'd be the right thing, too.

The man looked at my clipboard, then at my X-rays. One of the doctors said something to him.

The man turned to him and said, 'Maybe.' Just that, quite softly, but it was enough to make the doctor look as if he wished he'd kept his mouth shut.

The man came over to my bed and stooped down. 'Hello, Lizzie,' he said. 'Can you hear me?'

I made a 'yes' noise.

He smiled. 'That's excellent, Lizzie. I'm Mr Robinson, your surgeon, and I'm going to have a look at that left leg of yours to see what we can do. Is that all right with you?'

I made another 'yes' noise. You know, I loved Mr Robinson already. No one had ever spoken that polite and posh to me before. I wasn't scared any more.

The examination hurt. Mr Robinson said he was sorry, but he needn't have done – I knew he was doing his best.

When he'd finished, he took off his rubber gloves, washed his hands and said, 'I'll be back in a moment, Lizzie. I have to make a quick phone call. Excuse me.'

Kate said I was a lucky girl because Mr Robinson was one of the best surgeons in the province. I thought he was *the* best. Till I met him, I'd seen people with manners like that only in old films.

★ ★ ★

I dozed off or passed out, and the next thing I remember was Mr Robinson sitting beside my bed. He was quite close to me and looking straight into my eyes.

'Ah! There we are,' he said. 'Good. Do you remember me, Lizzie? Mr Robinson.'

I tried to smile. Did he really think I was that stupid?

He smiled back. 'Splendid, Lizzie! Now, listen carefully. Your left leg has been badly damaged, very badly damaged. I won't bore you with the details, but it's not going to be easy putting it back together again. I'm going to have a go tonight. I've spoken to your parents and they want me to tell you what I told them. I'm sure they're right, Lizzie.' He glanced at Kate.

'Now, there's a chance, quite a strong chance unfortunately, that I'll not be able to save your leg. I won't be able to tell for certain until we're in theatre.' He was looking straight at me, his brown eyes wide and unblinking. 'I'm very sorry, Lizzie, and I wish it wasn't so, but if things are in the state I think they are, I'll have to amputate – that is, remove the part of your leg that can't be repaired.'

## *Fifteen*

# Sunday, 10.12

Since my operations I've spoken to loads of people who've also had them. They all say the same thing: the last thing you remember is a nurse telling you you'll feel sleepy . . . then nothing. It was like that with me.

I hadn't really taken in what Mr Robinson had told me. I was only half awake and it was such a big thing that it probably wouldn't have registered straight off even if I'd been fresh as a daisy. Besides, when your whole world has been blown up and shattered into a million pieces, there are no more surprises. Your brain just says 'Oh, yes?' to everything, like it's had enough and stopped bothering.

So when I came round, I didn't straight away think, Oh, my God! I hope my leg's OK! To tell the truth, I'd forgotten all about what Mr Robinson had said, and even about the bomb and where I was.

I lay there, half in dreams and half out. Like oil in a

puddle, dreams and real life made patterns without mixing: a bit of dream about me riding a zebra through the school hall and the head timing me with a watch that went bleep, bleep, bleep . . . then a voice that sounded like Mum . . . then the zebra and the watch again . . . then Dad saying something . . .

'Hello, Lizzie, love. We're here!' He was quieter, softer than usual. I was glad he didn't try and make a joke.

'Oh, Lizzie, my darling girl!' said Mum. She sounded like she was crying.

I opened my eyes. The first thing I saw was this mountain in front of me, a soft, cream-coloured mountain. Then I looked up and saw all these tubes and wires coming out of me – it was like being in the middle of the chemistry lab when the sixth form were working there. The bleep noise was not the head's watch but some instrument behind me.

Beyond the mountain, the tubes and the wires, were two faces. Mum and Dad – my mum and dad! They looked wrecked.

Mum was crying. She came forward and stroked my hand. All she could say was 'Lizzie, oh, Lizzie!' Dad hung about behind the mountain, looking lost and worried.

I slept a bit more and when I woke up, they were still there. Mum put her finger in a plastic cup of water and wet my lips. It was lovely!

'More!' I croaked.

'I'm sorry, love,' said Mum, 'but the nurse says you mustn't drink yet.'

'Where am I?' I asked.

'Intensive care,' said Mum. 'It's a special ward for patients that need looking after all the time.' She gave a sort of smile and said, 'You're very special, Lizzie!' Then she started crying again.

Dad moved round to her side of the bed and put his arms round her. A nurse came up and said it was best if I had a bit of peace and quiet now. Mum and Dad nodded and got up to go.

'What's that?' I asked.

Mum didn't know what I was on about. 'What's what, my love?'

'The mountain thing, over the bottom of the bed?'

Mum looked at Dad. He looked at the mountain and, without taking his eyes off it, said, 'It's to keep the sheets and blankets off your operation.'

'Ah!' I said. 'Leg still hurts.'

Dad looked at me quickly. 'Is that so? Yes, I expect it will for a bit yet. Just you have a rest now. Mum and I will be back soon. 'Bye, Lizzie darling!'

He couldn't kiss me because of the tubes and things, so he just gave my hand a little squeeze.

* * *

A nurse called Yvonne woke me up some time later and said she was going to check me over. She was cheery and quick, like a gym teacher. When she asked if I was in pain and I said 'yes', she didn't say she was sorry or anything like that; she just said she'd try and do something about it. I reckon working in intensive care had squeezed a lot of gentleness out of her. For a start, she called me 'Elizabeth', not 'Lizzie' like everyone else.

Yvonne took my temperature, checked my drips and the tube for my wee, and gave me a tiny drop of water to drink. She looked over the dressings on my face, my arms and the front of my body. It hadn't really registered till then that I'd been hurt other than in my left leg. Now I was starting to think a bit straighter and I wanted to know more.

'What are all those dressings for, nurse?'

'You were very badly cut, Elizabeth. Flying glass, probably. It's unpleasant stuff.' She moved down the bed and looked under the mountain.

'Was my right leg hurt, too?'

'Yes, it was.'

I thought she gave a short answer because she was busy. Now I know it was because she didn't want to talk about it.

'And my left one?' I asked. 'It still hurts. The doctor – you know, the kind one with the posh voice – he said something about saving it. I can't remember.'

Yvonne put the covers back over the mountain. 'Mr Robinson will come and see you in the morning, Elizabeth. He'll tell you himself what he did.'

She tucked me up and gave me an injection. I fell asleep before I could think about what she had said to me.

*Sixteen*

# Monday, 10.15

Mum told me Mr Robinson came to see me a couple of times when I was asleep. She liked him as much as I did. 'A real gentleman,' she said he was.

My leg was still hurting a lot on Monday morning and I found I had new pains in lots of other places. But I was less woozy. They had switched off the bleeper, too, which meant they didn't think I was going to die on them all of a sudden. One of the nurses said I'd most likely be going to a normal ward on Tuesday.

Mum and Dad came in after breakfast. They said they'd been staying in a bed and breakfast place and the woman who ran it was very kind when she heard about me and the bombing and all that. Vicky was with Auntie Sue and Uncle Ian. She had a broken arm, but that was all, thank God. She'd been standing right next to me when the bomb went off, so I must have sheltered her from the blast.

That's how we got on to talking about the bomb, by accident. I could feel they didn't want to say much, and Dad tried to change the subject.

'Nurses OK to you, Lizzie?' he asked.

I said they were great and asked about the bomb again. There were so many things I wanted to know. Most of all, now that I knew Vicky was safe, I wanted to know about someone else. The boy who'd been standing right next to the car when it blew up . . . I couldn't ask about that, though. Instead, I said, 'Who did it, Dad?'

'Who did what, Lizzie?'

'The bomb.'

'Of course. Sorry. Well, no one's taken responsibility. They wouldn't, would they? But we all know it was them bloody cowardly Catholic—'

Mum put her hand on his arm. Mr Robinson had come in and was standing behind them. 'Good morning, Mr and Mrs McCallum,' he said. 'Good morning, Lizzie. How's our patient today?'

Mum said I was feeling better.

'Then perhaps this is a good time for me to have a word with Lizzie on my own?' said Mr Robinson. Mum and Dad agreed and said they'd wait outside.

Mr Robinson sat in the chair Mum had been in, on my

left. He looked very tired. The dark rings under his eyes were even bigger through his glasses.

'I'm glad you're feeling better, Lizzie,' he said. I remembered his soft voice from the last time he spoke to me. 'Now, when you were brought in here I explained what I was going to do. You were heavily sedated so probably not much of it sunk in. Am I right?'

'You said something about what a mess my leg was. You were going to try to make it better, I think.'

'That was about it, Lizzie, yes. Well, your parents have asked me to explain how we got on.'

It was starting to become clearer now, like something familiar coming out of a fog. The trouble was, I didn't want to recognize it.

'The blast from the bomb caught you head on, that's why most of your injuries are on the front of your body.' I thought of the dressings on my arms and stomach. 'You were badly cut in many places, Lizzie, almost certainly from flying glass. However, something larger and heavier than a piece of glass – perhaps a bit of the car bodywork – caught you on . . .'

No need to say it, doctor, I thought. On my left leg. The leg that I saw when I looked down just after the explosion. The torn bits of jeans, the blood . . .

'Would you like something to drink, Lizzie?'

'No, it's OK doctor. I was just thinking, that's all.'

'Of course.' He was looking at me with such kind eyes, as if he was looking at his own daughter. When his mouth gave a funny sort of twitch, I suddenly realized that he was finding this harder than me.

'Go on,' I said.

'You probably know what I'm going to say, don't you, Lizzie?'

'Yes. Well, no. What is it, doctor?' Of course I knew, but I wanted to hear it from him.

'I'll need to operate on your left leg again, I'm afraid, but when we've finished I'm pretty confident it will work just about normally above the knee. But not below that. The limb was so badly damaged from the knee downwards that I'm afraid we had no choice but to amputate. Take it off. I'm very, very sorry, Lizzie.'

Of course I'd known it ever since I'd seen the mountain on the bed and the look in Mum and Dad's faces. Now it was up front, no hiding: I was handicapped, disadvantaged, special needs, whatever.

So what did I think after the doctor had given it to me straight? Nothing. I was numb, brain dead.

Mr Robinson was still speaking but I couldn't hear him. The only thing in my mind was, Where was it, that bit of my leg? Where'd they put my shin, my foot, my toes? You can't just lose something like that, can you? It can't just be chucked away!

I was crying and Mr Robinson turned round to call for a nurse. As he did so, something slipped out of the front of his shirt. Something silver, on a silver chain. It was a tiny crucifix with a figure of Jesus on it.

In many places it wouldn't have mattered. But where I come from it was everything. A crucifix meant only one thing: Mr Robinson was Roman Catholic.

Mr Robinson and a nurse called Sandra were really kind. They sat with me till I'd calmed down, then they started explaining things I needed to know.

Mr Robinson said it was normal to feel pain in a limb that wasn't there. 'One of nature's little tricks,' he said.

When I asked about wheelchairs, he smiled and said I'd never need one. Sandra agreed with him. She said I'd learn to walk so well that no one would ever know the bottom bit of my left leg wasn't mine.

'Except my husband!' I said.

That made them laugh. I laughed, too.

Things were OK till Mum and Dad came back. Then the tears started all over again. Mum cried as soon as she saw me, so I started up. Even Dad had to look away and dry his eyes on his shirt sleeve.

Mr Robinson left when Mum had calmed down a bit. 'That's what I call a real gentleman,' she said as he walked out of the doors. 'You don't see manners like that these days.'

Dad agreed. I thought maybe I should tell them about the crucifix but I decided not to. It wasn't worth it. Anyway, I didn't know then what to make of it myself.

I wasn't crying now. The slightest thing set me off, though, like when Dad said Vicky had phoned. She had asked about me a lot, he said, and Auntie Sue had taken her to get the shoes she didn't get on Saturday . . .

Dad hadn't meant to upset me, but when he said 'shoes', like a pair, one for each foot . . . well, I just howled. A bit later Sandra gave me an injection to calm me down and Mum and Dad went back to their bed and breakfast place.

## *Seventeen*

# Tuesday, 09.27

On Tuesday morning they moved me out of the intensive care to a children's ward. As Sandra was getting me ready, I asked her if Mr Robinson was a Catholic.

'What a funny question, Lizzie!' she said. 'We don't have such things in here, you know. We're just people: doctors, nurses, paramedics and so on.'

'You mean you don't know?' I asked.

Sandra stopped what she was doing. 'What's it to you, Lizzie?'

'Dad says it was Catholics that set off the bomb, so I sort of hope it's a Catholic that's making me better. It'd cancel things out, if you know what I mean.'

'Yes, I think I know,' said Sandra. 'I'm not supposed to say this, but if it helps . . . Yes, I think Mr Robinson is a Roman Catholic. At least, my husband and I are and he sometimes turns up at our church.'

I'm surrounded by them, I thought. Mr Robinson *and* Sandra – maybe Kate and my guardian angel were Catholics, too? There was no way of telling. What's more, they had all been really good to me. They'd smiled, like Patrick had smiled, just before the bomb . . .

I couldn't get my mind round it. The whole stupid thing – Catholic and Protestant, Nationalist and Unionist – wasn't easy like when Dad had made sarky remarks at the news. It wasn't just 'them' and 'us', was it? Like my leg had been, it was just a bloody mess.

They put me in the bed next to the door in a small children's ward. Just three beds in it but they closed the curtains round mine so I couldn't see the others. Tracy was opposite. She'd had her appendix out and was waiting to go home. She spent most of the time in the TV room down the corridor.

Alex, in the bed next to me, was having some sort of radiotherapy. She didn't seem much bothered about it.

'Are you Lizzie?' she asked when the nurse had gone.

'Yes.' I was tired and hurting all over. I didn't feel like talking.

'I'm Alex. You were in the bomb, then?'

'Suppose so.'

'Bastards they are! Can I have a look?'

I didn't say anything but I heard her getting out of bed and pulling back the curtains between us. 'Jesus! They did that to you?'

I hadn't thought much about what I looked like. I suppose, with all those stitches in my face and half my hair shaved off to get at the cuts on my head, I wouldn't have won a beauty contest.

'I'm tired, Alex,' I said.

'Sure. Sorry, Lizzie!' I heard her getting back into bed. 'Even so,' she went on, 'they're bastards, you know. Bloody Fenian bastards! I hate 'em all!'

My eyes were closed. I thought of Mum and Dad, Mr Robinson and Sandra, and a boy with bright green eyes . . .

'I said I hate 'em!' repeated Alex.

'I heard,' I said. 'But I don't.'

'You're mad!'

I was almost asleep. 'Maybe,' I muttered. 'But I think it's better like that.'

## *Eighteen*

# Wednesday 10.25

Dad went home on Tuesday. He had to get back to work. Mum stayed on and came to see me on Wednesday morning. Tracy was watching TV in the lounge and Alex was having her treatment, so we had the ward all to ourselves.

The mountain was still over my legs and they hadn't let me look underneath it yet. Even so, I felt better than I'd done since the operation. I had only one drip now and some of my wounds had started to itch, which the nurses said was a good sign.

'Your hair's growing back already,' said Mum. You'll be able to wash it soon.'

'Not till the stitches are out.'

'Won't be long.' Mum opened her bag and took out a little box. 'Here,' she said, 'something to cheer you up.'

It was perfume, real French stuff. I'd never had anything

like that before. Never even smelt it. Mum took off the top and dabbed a bit on my arm, the one without the drip in it. The scent was magic – I'd never known a smell say so much. It was like a message from a fantasy land.

'That's great, Mum! Brilliant!' I said. 'Thanks. But you shouldn't have spent all that.'

Mum looked at me as if she could love me to bits. 'I know, Lizzie. But I wanted you to have something that's different from all this.' She waved her hand around the ward. 'I thought you could do with a wee bit of luxury after what you've been through. Won't do any harm, will it?'

'No. But you're spoiling me,' I said. 'It's not right. Just because, well, just because . . .' I didn't know what to say.

'I'm not spoiling you, Lizzie,' said Mum. 'It's a celebration. You're still with us. Think what could have happened.'

Neither of us spoke for a bit. 'So what did happen?' I asked. 'Were lots of people killed?'

'Twenty-six, twenty-eight – I don't know. More than any bomb in the whole of the Troubles. Not just Protestants, either. Lots of their own side.'

'You mean Catholics?'

'I mean Catholics, Lizzie. Like that Patrick O'Brien, the

boy that gave you the trouble in Carson Street. How d'you think his mum's feeling now?'

*Patrick!* My eyes started filling up with tears. Through them, gleaming like jewels, I saw again those bright green eyes.

'Worse than you, I reckon. He was the same age as me. Remember what you said about us young having everything to live for?'

'Of course.'

'Everything?' I asked.

'Why not?'

I looked at her to see if she meant it. I couldn't tell. 'Not quite everything,' I said.

She didn't argue.

# Historical Notes

The Omagh bombing shocked the world. Twenty-nine people were killed and 220 injured. The victims included tourists and visitors as well as the citizens of Omagh. The slaughter was all the more distressing because, officially, there had been a cease-fire in Northern Ireland since 1994 and there was a general mood of optimism following the Good Friday Agreement.

After the bombing, all paramilitary groups confirmed that they were on cease-fire. The authorities set about tracking down those who had committed the crime. Before long they had a fair idea who was responsible, but they did not have enough evidence to bring them to court.

In the meantime, the Agreement was accepted by the citizens of Eire and Northern Ireland. After further problems, on 2 December 1999 Northern Ireland became self-governing with an elected assembly in which power was shared between the Nationalists (Catholics) and Loyalists (Protestants). All paramilitary groups were to disarm by May 2000.

When the date came, not a single weapon had been handed in. A year later, on the third anniversary of the Omagh bombing, nothing had changed. In the autumn of 2001, news came through of a breakthrough: the IRA had put some weapons permanently beyond use. It was only a gesture, but it was a significant one. A small step towards resolution. Meanwhile, as the talking continued, on the streets the violence began to flare up again, fanned by the wind of age-old hatreds . . .

*Timeline:*

# The Divided Island

| | |
|---|---|
| 1171 | King Henry II of England invades Ireland. Most of the country comes under his authority. |
| 1541 | Henry VIII of England proclaims himself King of Ireland. |
| 1552 | First English Protestant bishops appointed to Ireland, a largely Catholic country. |
| 1557 | First plantation (settlement with Protestant English and Scots immigrants) begins. |
| 1609 | Plantation of Ulster begins. In time this leads to a country divided between a largely Catholic south and a largely Protestant north. |
| 1641 | Massive Irish rebellion against English overlords. |
| 1649 | Oliver Cromwell restores English rule. |
| 1689–90 | William of Orange relieves the Catholic siege of Derry and defeats the Catholic James II at the Battle of the Boyne. |

| | |
|---|---|
| 1800 | Act of Union: British and Irish parliaments are united. |
| 1845–50 | About 1 million Irish people die in the potato famine. Huge numbers of people emigrate. |
| 1860s | Irish Home Rule movement gathering strength. Some groups use terrorist tactics. |
| 1886 | Gladstone's government fails to get an Irish Home Rule Bill through parliament. |
| 1912 | Liberal government's Irish Home Rule Bill moves through parliament. |
| 1914 | Irish Home Rule shelved with outbreak of First World War. |
| 1916 | British put down Nationalist 'Easter Rising' rebellion in Dublin. |
| 1920 | Fighting breaks out as Ulster refuses to be part of a future Irish state. |
| 1921 | Anglo-Irish Treaty grants independence to southern Ireland (Eire). |
| 1922 | Irish Republican Army (IRA) rejects Anglo-Irish Treaty. |
| 1930s | Sporadic IRA violence. |
| 1968 | Attempts by government of Northern Ireland to end anti-Catholic discrimination there. |
| 1969 | Widespread violence between Protestants and Catholics in Northern Ireland. |

| | |
|---|---|
| | British Army called in. Beginning of the 'Troubles' that kill over 3,000 people by 1990s. |
| 1998 | Good Friday Agreement between Protestants and Catholics of Northern Ireland brings prospect of lasting peace. Omagh bombing. |
| 1999 | Northern Ireland becomes self-governing under an assembly that shares power between Protestants and Catholics. |
| 2001 | Some IRA weapons put beyond use. |

# Further Information

There are very few children's books on the subject of Northern Ireland, but the following may be useful:

Grant, R.G., *Lives in Crisis: Conflict in Northern Ireland* (Hodder Wayland, 2001)

Minnis, Ivan, *Northern Ireland* (Heinemann, 2001)

The Omagh story is told in painful detail and with honest clarity on www.irelandstory.com/past/omagh

# Glossary

**Amputate** To cut off a part of the body because of injury or disease.

**Antichrist** The devil.

**Assembly** A meeting of parliament.

**Cease-fire** An agreement to stop fighting temporarily.

**Civil rights** Rights, such as freedom of speech and the right to vote, that people expect in a free country.

**Eire** The official name of the Irish Republic.

**Fenian** The slang name for a Catholic (or Nationalist) in Northern Ireland. It comes from the name of a nineteenth-century gang that used violence to try to win Irish independence from Britain.

**Freedom Fighter** A controversial term for someone who uses violence to try to win independence. One person's 'freedom fighter' is another person's 'terrorist'.

**Good Friday Agreement** An agreement (also called the

Belfast Agreement) signed on Good Friday 1998 between the Protestants and Catholics of Northern Ireland. It established the principle that the province should be ruled by an assembly in which power was shared between the two communities.

**Intensive care** A hospital ward for patients whose lives are in immediate danger.

**IRA** The Irish Republican Army, a group dedicated to winning a united, independent Ireland.

**Loyalist** A member of the Protestant community of Northern Ireland who wishes the province to remain part of the United Kingdom.

**Major trauma** Serious bodily injury and shock.

**Militant** A person that is prepared to fight to achieve an aim (usually political).

**Nationalist** A member of the Catholic community of Northern Ireland who wishes the province to be part of a united, independent Ireland.

**Paramilitary** Belonging to an unofficial and illegal military-style group.

**Provisional IRA** A branch of the IRA.

**Radiotherapy** The treatment of cancer and other illnesses by X-rays or other forms of radiation.

**Terrorist** Someone who uses violence to achieve a political aim.

**The Troubles** Sectarian (Protestant v. Catholic) turmoil in Northern Ireland, 1968–?.

**Ulster** The Protestant name for Northern Ireland, although, strictly speaking, Ulster is an area slightly bigger than Northern Ireland, and also includes the counties of Cavan, Donegal and Monaghan, which are in Eire.

**Unionist** Someone who wishes Northern Ireland (Ulster) to remain part of the United Kingdom.

**Viewfinder** The part of a camera that shows the area that will appear in a photograph.